ARE YOU MY DAD?

By Leslie Kelley

Illustrations by Kirk Werner

First published by Dog Ear Publishing
4011 Vincennes Rd
Indianapolis, IN 46268
www.dogearpublishing.net

ISBN: 978-1-4575-5885-6

This book is printed on acid-free paper.

This book is a work of fiction. Places, events, and situations in this book are purely fictional and any resemblance to actual persons, living or dead, is coincidental.

Printed in the United States of America

An egg sat snuggled on her dad's feet. The baby bird inside leaned her egg to the left. She wriggled it to the right. She twisted it backward and tilted it forward. Then she rolled her egg right off her dad's feet and down a small hill! A gust of wind pushed her egg and it rolled down a BIG hill.

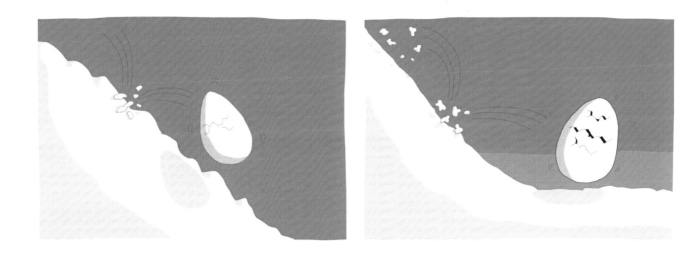

Down, down, down her egg traveled until out she popped!
"Where is my dad?" she asked. She looked left. She peered right. She glanced behind and gazed in front.

"My dad is lost!" she cried. "I must go and find him," and away she went.

Down a snowy slope she slipped.   Over an icy ridge she slid.

Along a cold path she waddled, to the edge of a hill where she saw an albatross.

"Are *you* my dad?" she yelled.

The albatross looked down at her and replied, "I am a bird like your dad, but he swims in the sea and cannot fly like me!" and away he flew. The baby bird waddled on.

Around a snowy rise she slipped.

Under an icy ledge she slid.

Beside a cold trail she wandered, until she came to the edge of the sea
where she spied an orca.

"Are *you* my dad?" she yelled.

The orca squinted at her and replied, "I swim like your dad, but he lives on land while I live in the sea, and he is *much* smaller than me!" and away he swam with a grand splash. The baby bird shook herself off and waddled on.

Beyond a snowy bank she slipped.

Past an icy bridge she slid.

Between cold tracks she wiggled until she came upon an elephant seal.

"Are *you* my dad?" she asked.

The seal paused and then replied, "I have flippers like your dad. I swim in the sea but live on land like your dad, and though some say he is tall, he is still *small* compared to me!" and he wiggled into the sea. The baby bird slipped on with her head hung low.

"My dad is *very* lost. Where can he be?!" she worried and began to waddle faster...

She passed a blue whale spouting water.

She spied a fur seal lazing in the sun.

She saw a tern flying near a hill... "None of *you* can be my dad..." she grumbled.

Just then the baby bird noticed a strange something climbing out of the sea... The something knew how to swim but was resting on land. He had flippers but did not seem to know how to fly. He was not very small and he was *definitely* tall...

"Dad? Dad?! DAD! I found you!" she squealed.

The strange something stopped and turned toward the peeping baby bird. He lifted an object to his face and began clicking madly.

The baby bird halted. "Uh-oh! You are not my dad. *You* are a clicker!" she screeched as it began slowly moving toward her. The baby bird turned, waddled, slipped, and slid as fast as she could away from the clicker.

Quickly past the tern, the seal, and the whale she went.

ong the cold path she slid, away from the elephant seal.

Over the icy ridge she waddled away from the orca and the sea.

Up the snowy slope she slipped, away from the soaring albatross.

Over, around, between, and up, up, up she waddled until finally, she reached the top.

There, all around her were emperor penguin dads with baby birds nestled on their feet.
Off to one side was a dad with his head hung low.

19

She waddled right over to him and stated, "I know *you*. You are a bird who cannot fly. You live on land but swim in the sea. You're rather tall, and you've been missing me!"

The daddy emperor penguin opened his eyes wide and smiled a BIG smile. With a contented sigh and a twinkle in his eye, he snuggled his precious baby penguin onto his feet and held on tightly, while in the distance a strange thing clicked madly...

CPSIA information can be obtained
at www.ICGtesting.com
Printed in the USA
BVXC01n0407241017
498056BV00004B/24

9 781457 558856